Stories

From Someone
Older Than Television

Enjoy

Margie Zats

Share the fun!

www.margiesmarvelousmunchies.com

Dedicated to my Fabulous Five

This book is for: _____

_____

From: _____

_____

CONTENTS

Lightbulb   *1*

Home On the Range—
and I Don't Mean the Old West   *5*

My Life as a Car   *11*

The Blue Sky Boutique   *19*

A Touch of Glass   *27*

Cordial Means More Than "Hello"   *33*

Back When "Cable" Meant a Telegram   *43*

Red, White and Sometimes Blue   *51*

Innovative Inventions   *57*

Life Savers   *67*

A Short Sport Report   *75*

Counter Intelligence   *83*

Smaller Is Better   *91*

I'll Be Seeing You. . .   *95*

Recipes   *99*

For years, I've had opinions nobody ever asked me about.

I'm not hounded by the *paparazzi* or contacted by the news media. Not even the neighbor's dog chases me. I'm just a regular person living on a tree-lined city block.

However, because I've been around the block many times, I've been observing and pondering—arriving at medium-bright conclusions.

It occurs to me you've been thinking about many of the same subjects and have had similar experiences.

So with the help of a small, cheap Boom Box, Rod Stewart joins me at the kitchen table and I now put a ballpoint pen to these reflections.

My initial thought is cosmetic: How he appears on stage with the same hairstyle I awaken with.

He disarms the clock-ticking silence with a raspy "Embraceable You." The young girl deep inside me longs to be free to dance again. Her mature counterpart wonders if he has polyps on his vocal cords.

No matter. The mood is set. And, as in a Stardust Melody, I am once again with you.

I hope these stories embrace you, gentle reader.

I hope they'll be an incentive to give away a smile—and relax a little more tonight.

I hope you find, within these pages, a laugh—and a new old friend.

Margie

HOME ON THE RANGE
AND *I DON'T MEAN THE OLD WEST*

Some night I'll see myself on the six p.m. news.

That's the program with the Human Interest Stories about lost puppies, stolen charity money and people who live in unusual places. Like cardboard boxes.

Only my scenario is different. I live in the kitchen. My days into evenings are engulfed in Corion and coriander. Yes, there are other rooms in the house and a nice hallway, too, leading out to the Free World. But, I must stay back and keep the unmatched cookware company.

This is not a cry for compassion. It's simply that the life of a pastry chef is sometimes bittersweet, and not necessarily, dipped in ganache.

The day begins with the ritual of over-watering my plants (don't write me about this.) I then decipher the bulletin board.

Orders are checked and each cookie flavor is made. Chocolate chips consistently outnumber anything with raisins. High fiber comes in pitifully low.

Basic rule: The funny-looking cookies must be consumed while still warm. I regard this as an act of mercy. Poor mounds, lying there like wounded soldiers on a battlefield of waxed paper.

With energy from a heightened blood sugar level, I proceed.

The ovens are heated. And so am I. Off comes the sweatshirt. On goes the Tee embossed with a slogan I can't wear in public.

The boom box booms. No sounds of the surf, please. A brass section sets the mood. Fortunately, I don't specialize in Viennese pastries as I am incapable of beating the batter in three-quarters time.

The pans are sprayed with non-stick aerosol. Great care is taken to protect the collection of faux Monets on a nearby wall. By this time my apron has an abstract design never before seen on the fashion runways of Paris. Each cover-up is, amazingly, a one-of-a-kind. Every day, a bottle of vanilla tips at a different angle, powdered sugar randomly tickles the hemline and sticky fingers embellish the bodice. Givenchy would be astounded at my cook's couture. Or should I say, he'd be "frosted."

But this artistry exceeds my persona. While my technique may differ from Jackson Pollack's, I, too, create on the floor. A masterpiece underfoot and underwhelming. Though mine is not museum quality it certainly is transient. Destined for a wet sponge. A mixed media of eggshells, dough clumps and puddles of cream provoke the viewer into an immediate emotional response: watch where you walk.

I've memorized each groove in the cutting board. The little blue diamonds of the Congoleum dance in my slumber. The purple clock shows me how many faces will behold a mid-morning snack. Countless cups of coffee are enriched by wonderful empty calories.

How many grumbling mouths will soon turn upwards into a grin? All because of a meaningful carb.

Every time I look at me I'm in the same place.

The island counter is my center of gravity. Of course I leave, say to go the dentist. But, I come right back. As if drawn by an invisible magnet.

If I could sing an aria, I'd hole up in a French garret. If I had long golden tresses a hidden tower would be home. Perhaps a small cottage on the edge of the forest would suffice a poet.

But those are not options for one who bakes banana bread.

On occasion the refrigerator hums in the key of B-Flat and the egg timer clicks rhythmically as if cueing a flamenco dancer. The mixer adds a pulsating whirl while the tap water trickles in lush undertones.

My culinary concerto commences.

The aroma of fudge revel and warm toffee swirl about, infusing the room in luxury.

All who enter succumb.

If only it could be bottled. And sold by-the-sniff.

Four walls make a room. But a kitchen, brimming with good things to eat, makes a memory.

I guess that's why I stay.

Bon appétit.

MY LIFE AS A CAR

A spontaneous thought occurred to me: My life has been chronicled by my seat in the car.

This is not to be compared with living life by the seat of my pants.

It truly means getting into an automobile. Where I sit translates to who I am at the moment and what I can expect from the road ahead. It is a visible diary for every passerby to clearly read.

The journey begins as a passenger within a passenger totally embodied in Mother and unaware of the exhilaration aboard.

You, the oblivious rider, are nestled beneath a coat that won't button, ignorant to the sounds of the night and the desperate need for destination.

Front seat, back seat, who cares? It's the drive of a lifetime. Literally, it is Life Time.

The route back home from Stork Town is, however, quite different. You're on your own. Already relegated to the back seat.

And if that demotion isn't enough, you're confined in some sort of contraption without a view.

Trees and billboards everywhere and nothing to see. Immaterial. True, your eyes cannot yet focus, but it's the principle that matters.

Give a holler. It won't help. The law insists you be strapped into this apparatus.

You're not sure what the "law" is but it must taste terrible because the grown-ups get a funny look on their faces whenever they say the word.

And so the infant years and the toddler car seat eventually pass. But they don't pass you by because you're still stuck in the back seat. Only now it's worse 'cuz you're also stuck with your kid brother and bossy sister. One hits and grabs your Game Boy and the other whines on cue.

No amount of complaining or negotiating helps because this "law" thing sentences you to twelve years.

Only by eating excessive Ding Dongs can you expedite your placement by increasing your weight to one hundred pounds.

Once accomplished you can get on the Option Plan: One adult, one kid (meaning you) equals the Front Seat.

This opportunity is valid for most Saturday mornings and school drop-offs.

Family outings and special guests are excluded. You're back to the back.

This vacillation continues for a number of years until you attain the magical One Five. And then, a drum roll please—excerpts from the Grande Marche from Aida emanate from the heavens. It's Driver's Training Time.

American Royalty is at the wheel.

Not only are you in the Front Seat, but—get this—you are grasping the steering wheel. Mother Love. The sky has opened and you are its brightest star.

As you are now an almost Registered Driver, everyone in the five-state area, or at least your high school, should revere the accomplishment.

Trophies have been won by many but only you, in the history of the world, own that stare on a state-issued piece of plastic.

With the sheer joy of weekend parties, however, comes the burden of everyday errands. Not yours. Everyone else's.

Pick up milk, drop off laundry, get sister at dance class. Take her friends home, too.

Why, you ask, does every rose have a thorn? If we knew that, we'd go on to the meaning of life.

Just get back in the car.

Years whiz by and you've managed your own wheels. Chairman of the Dash Board. But now you've got to fill 'er up, wash it down and pay some ridiculous insurance company whose tables were formulated by anti-youth sadists.

We're back to the roses.

In a vernacular I don't quite grasp, a paradox appears: You're hot because your wheels are cool. Or maybe it's the other way around.

Whatever—you have now accelerated to the Fast Lane.

Oh, but Love is larger than a limousine. No longer are you the exclusive driver but willingly glide across, on occasion, to the passenger side. Ousted with no regret.

The road ahead is clear and in your heart you know you're still in the driver's seat.

As the years fill, so does the back seat. With carseats and multiple pestering.

Your body's partially in front but your head is on continual swivel to quell the screams of who spilled what on whom.

An entire soccer team issues a disclaimer.

You remind yourself driving and drinking don't mix.

Then one day that last kid drives off to school and/or the job in the city.

The car becomes silent. The CD's of artists long off the charts fill the front, leaving the bass tones to serenade a bag of non-fat/non-flavor groceries.

The dependable servant is filled with golf clubs, expandable luggage on wheels and assorted paraphernalia of choice.

Strange though, the front seat keeps getting higher. Perhaps a back cushion would suffice.

Your four-door friend seems to drive a little slower, too. And not so much at night. Or in bad weather.

But, you're still in the front seat and loving it.

Then there's the weekend the kids come to visit. Dinner at the club. Your treat.

Everyone, brilliant and gorgeous grandchildren included, run to the driveway.

"Maybe you'd be more comfortable in the back, Mom," is softly said.

"Here, Dad, it's easier to get in. Let me help you."

And the cycle of life follows a familiar road.

You're back where you began. In the backseat. Hoping to get a window.

It's odd how a hunk of metal—a product not necessarily made in America—becomes a metaphor, an accounting of your life's journey.

How can that thing in the garage that needs washing provoke thought?

But it does.

My mind raced with similes: unexpected detours, difficult visibilities. We could go on 'til midnight drawing parallels.

But you've got it.

Along with my good wishes: that you slow down once in a while, notice the flowers alongside the road, and above all, enjoy the ride.

The Blue Sky Boutique

There must be shopping in heaven 'cuz that's how it got its name. Having earned my Black Belt in belts, shoes and bags, I wasn't leaving anything to chance. Yearning to spend my "here-after" browsing in shoppers' paradise, I explored my options. How could I best secure eternity in angels' *ready-to-wear?* What strings would I have to pull?

I needed a direct route. Genetics. I could draw upon Grandpa Charlie. He who began the dynasty of Dark Brown eyes and an ear for melody.

Up until then, the only wings I was familiar with belonged on those spicy little hors d'oeuvres.

I wanted assurance. And I found it in my DNA.

Grandpa Charlie played the fiddle by ear. Hum a tune and a harmonica would spontaneously appear from one part of his three-piece suit. He played best if toe tapping was included.

And we, too, tapped and clapped and laughed until tears glistened in everybody's dark brown eyes.

Talent of this caliber could only occur every other generation, so I was a candidate. However, it zigzagged...to my brother.

Crowds would gather, three-deep, around the piano as he'd play...any song in any key...to which anyone could remember the lyrics. The quality of vocalizing improved in direct ratio to the quantity of glasses on top of the piano.

They kept the windows closed at many a fraternity party. By midnight auditions could have been held for musical theater.

This joviality made me think: Though Grandpa may have preferred male heirs, I most certainly was educable.

I can't remember if clouds parted and I got a message from above or a Harpo Marx movie caught my attention. But one day in June, I decided to become a harpist.

I found a teacher who accepted the challenge.

My son came with for my first lesson, which I told him was only fair as I'd taken him to school his first day. I reinforced my logic with a pan of brownies.

But I needn't have been apprehensive. The teacher was kind and the instrument gorgeous and gold-plated. It outweighed me, too.

She told me to sit. I thought I could ride the thing side-saddle. I soon, however, purchased a new wardrobe of wide-legged pants.

My mother never adjusted.

Practice makes perfect…which eluded me. But being totally sincere and hard-working, I improved.

My fingertips became so callused from the *glissandos* (shimmering the octaves) that to my delight I could remove hot bagels from the toaster without flinching.

I offered to do this for everyone in the family.

Fundamental kiddie songs matured to Mozart and eventually I was ready for community orchestra.

The conductor was astounded when I appeared. Not because of my ability, but the law of supply and demand worked in my favor.

There isn't a lot of harp players around.

The instrument is expensive and difficult to learn. It's something like playing the piano from the inside.

Another problem: Transportation. At one glance I knew a concert harp wouldn't fit alongside the groceries in the trunk of the car. Rehearsals couldn't be held in my living room, so with one clever purchase I solved the dilemma: a small recorder. I'd put the entire program on tape, then come home, press the "ON" button and pluck away. What a plan.

The one drawback was my dog. For reasons only a veterinarian could explain, Tiger the Shih Tzu was fascinated with the music. Perhaps only his sensitive ears could capture the illusive notes humans aren't privy to. The minute I'd begin he'd position himself by the "D" pedal until I played the final note.

Not wanting to hurt his feelings created a frustrating situation.

I couldn't ask him to move so I'd just maneuver around him. I didn't sound great. But I can't blame that on the dog.

I did discover, however, that even with both hands busy, I could eat while practicing. I developed a strategy for that, too.

If the cookie was perfectly round I was able to manipulate the edges, thereby rotating the circle until consumed. I would not, of course, do this during performances. Only in the late afternoon when hunger got the best of me.

For concerts I'd hire the maintenance man from the music store. He'd pick that harp up like I'd lift a muffin…and wait for me at the stage door. No, his name wasn't Johnny.

My first orchestral performance was about two thousand miles off Broadway.

I had Murphy's Law Stage Fright: anything that could go wrong would.

Again a plan.

The day before, I taped each sheet of music together in chronological order so I couldn't lose my place. When I'd finished, the whole stack rolled out to resemble a product commonly found in the ladies' room. I didn't care. I figured my method was foolproof.

But Murphy couldn't leave me alone.

I managed to get on stage without tripping and was grateful to be partially hidden by my instrument.

The conductor tapped his baton, the house lights diminished. A hush fell. And so did my confidence.

I should mention that a harpist does not play constantly; many composers just weren't into us, so my numbers were interspersed throughout the evening.

I was aghast. I had my pile of music, but I'd forgotten to get a program. There was no guide to tell me what song I was to play when.

I knew tomorrow my blouse would have to go to the laundry 'cuz I sure was going to the cleaners that night.

I saw my friend in the audience holding a program. It struck a chord. We had to communicate.

I slouched behind the harp and, somehow, conveyed a signal.

He read my expression.

First he'd scan the program, then, somewhat like Charades, he'd wave me a high-five sign.

That meant I was on. The strings were warmed up, and I pulled those puppies with all my heart.

The concert mercifully ended. I didn't make it to the reception.

One rehearsal the conductor informed us we were to participate in a city-wide event…a welcoming ceremony. I was to be the beach and re-create the swirls and swoops of the sand as new Americans sludged towards the promised shores.

Massive *glissandos* would fill the auditorium…resounding their achievement…and thickening my calluses. My mind flashed to all the bagels waiting to be toasted. I could feed the entire neighborhood. The moment of destiny arrived; the weary travelers left their boats. I pulled up and slid down. Up and down as imaginary immigrants trekked to freedom.

Each grain of sand became visible. You could almost feel the grit. And then…it was over.

I sat back, having reached the pinnacle of my musical ability.

Over the years, my melodious career continued…in staccato.

Once the recorder mysteriously broke as I taped my solo. I didn't realize sixteen bars were missing and couldn't figure out why Maestro kept pointing that stick at me during the concert.

Soon after that, I was put on tambourine. My assignment, during the Gypsy numbers, was to gently hit it on my right hip, immediately extending the disc over my head and proceed to shake it about. A toss of the hair was a nice accompaniment.

I practiced at home. The dog didn't wake up for this one.

I loved that orchestra, and they returned the affection. Particularly when I brought cookies.

Then, one autumn, the group didn't meet on the first Monday after Labor Day.

And the hours of my life became too crowded for practice. A harp must be played to stay in tune; the strings missed a gentle touch. It was time to sell. Besides, the "D" pedal looked lonely without a small dog alongside.

I found a buyer…and quickly left the room before my golden friend reached the doorway.

Now when I glimpse a poster of Harpo Marx I have to laugh at his goofy expression and that wondrous coat of many pockets.

The music wasn't dubbed, you know. He was genuine talent…and, I've read, a very good person. Perhaps he played his way to the sky.

It's anybody's guess.

Today I'm certain of only one truth: Harpo, like so many others, was not a natural blonde.

But that's another story.

A TOUCH OF GLASS

Blame it on Snow White, or that nasty Queen who had it in for her—and her talking mirror.

"Fairest in the Land" has become a familiar criteria. Some measurement of beauty influencing four-year-olds. To a preschooler the fable must be the best thing since double-dipping —released on both VHS and DVD.

As the story goes, though, it didn't do Snow much good to play house with seven men who came up to her knees.

At least she got a long snooze out of it. And, I'm sure, awakened looking very rested.

Too bad the apple industry couldn't launch an ad campaign based on the moral.

Then everybody would have been happy. Except the One formerly known as Queen.

Let's get back to this mirror thing.

Ever since the mythological Narcissus first gazed on his reflection in a pond, everyone's been curious about their appearance.

Stop and realize—you've actually never seen yourself.

Others view you 24/7 but you must depend on a visual aid. Unless, of course, you spend a lot of time pond-side.

A mirror can be its own entity. Or come as an added attraction—on a medicine cabinet, in a handbag, alongside a powder puff, even under a floral centerpiece.

Compose your own list if you're having trouble sleeping.

It can even do tricks such as tilt rear-view. Or ripple and curve in a Fun House so you appear 400 pounds heavier.

I don't want to discuss this anymore.

Mirrors can be harnessed in gold frames and decorated with ivy decals—which no one would believe was real because horticulture cannot grow on glass.

It is, however, a nice try.

A mirror can even be sprayed smoky. But then, what's the use of owning the thing when you can only recognize eyebrows.

In my opinion, the inventor of high density magnifying mirrors probably came up with the "windchill factor," too.

If I ever find him, it won't be pretty.

Smoke and mirrors, a technique originated by magicians to cloud and deceive, is applied daily to relationships. Particularly a favorite of prominent politicians and young men on weekends.

The best mirrors—the most compassionate—are the ones in poorly lit dressing rooms.

There, alone with a suit size you wore five years ago, old beauty can be recaptured.

I've heard there's a special light bulb made by Sylvania just for this purpose.

And sold, exclusively, to retailers. Bask in yesteryear's svelteness. They're waiting for you at the cash register.

If this is the top, you'll "bottom" out in a shower.

A contractor of dubious mentality must have designed the American bathroom. Head-to-toe mirrors steam up in the room. And so do you.

The impulse is to grab a towel and quickly start rubbing. But you can't rub off reality.

Only a well-toned movie star could surmount this inspection. And what would she be doing in your bathroom in the first place?

Trust me, call Sylvania.

As long as we've mentioned Hollywood, I've heard that some bon vivants have mirrors on their ceilings.

What's so special about that? I used to have a large one overhead as I demonstrated baking techniques in Cooking School.

A bun is a bun.

Constant involvement with our image isn't just vanity. To a philosopher a mirror is the reflection of the soul, that secret place within.

Gaze into the mystical looking glass and see your personal roadmap. It will be a welcome viewing of a familiar companion, a touching reminder of a stressful day.

This simple sheath of reflective material conveys many messages. It gives you the person you give the world.

Infused in every building, in nearly every room, everywhere we go, it's Look and Adjust.

Compulsive viewing maybe, but often pleasant. How preoccupied we are with cosmetic décor.

Fortune 500 companies have been built on Bad Hair Days, alone. When, of course, it's the mind underneath that counts.

Truthfully, nothing's going to change. We will never be able to pass a mirror without peeking.

This, however, does not apply to me. I am the lone exception.

But we'll have to talk later. I'm in a rush to get to the mall.

They're having a sale on Windex.

CORDIAL MEANS MORE
THAN "HELLO"

People have been grappling for grapes since history's been recorded.

With the sole exception of Mother's Milk, no other beverage has been so appreciated as the Nectar of the Gods.

Please note "divine" and "wine" rhyme. Coincidence?

I don't think so.

Our day begins as we open the newspaper to bold-faced ads of cellars sellers. We're invited to Happy Hour every Friday—a chance to sniff the bouquet of free samples—and have the reassurance that sometimes Full-Bodied is a good thing.

What other fluid has such fluidity? It's an art and a science combined. It's medicinal and romantic—and washes down *real nice*. A glass of the grape transports Venice, Italy, to Venice, California. Everyone is included.

It lowers blood pressure and inhibitions simultaneously.

A few drops on the mouth anesthetizes baby boys and soothes their first passage into manhood.

It spawns industry and provides a livelihood to a jillion people. Besides the obvious—the guy who makes bottle openers for a living—wine requires furniture to rack and stack it.

I recently came close to buying a four-foot metal man, presumably a French waiter, holding a removable tray. Presumably again, to pass the drinks. His trouser legs coiled into circles each securing six bottles of whatever you wanted. A nice conversation piece for shy guests. But the visual of chablis protruding from his thighs was worth less than the asking price.

The fashion industry increases sales simply by re-naming beige to "champagne" and maroon to "merlot." Today's "blush" refers to scant underwear—not the occupant's expression.

Even make-up is dubbed "burnished burgundy." Everybody's climbing on the oak barrel.

Wine probably began with Neanderthal man leaving berries back in the cave while he went trudging out to find a main course that didn't find him first.

Certainly there are numerous references from ancient Egypt. Imagine you're sipping the descendant of Cleopatra's apéritif.

Yes, throughout each century, every culture has paid homage to a vessel of vino.

When fruit wasn't available, seeds and bees were a honey of a concoction. That's how the term "honeymoon" began. Couples in Greece would drink a honey potion and, I suppose, gaze at the moon.

Makes a nice story.

While we're still in togas, late-night TV occasionally runs an epic Cecil B. DeMille extravaganza, resplendent with jewel-naveled dancing girls. Their cups never run over (I'm referring to the wine goblets) as they stealthily slither, with each drumbeat, towards their squinty-eyed emperor.

I'll never figure out how they managed to gyrate so precisely, never spilling a drop. Never stubbing a toe.

Conquerors transported plantings throughout Europe. In the evenings, it gave them pleasure to recline on an animal skin and unwind after a long day of pillaging and looting.

Before you could say "Spare me, Atilla," the countryside was a bloomin' vineyard.

Especially France, the acknowledged best, because they've been at it the longest. Even the geographical names are those of Grands Vins.

Thomas Jefferson brought back French "cuttings" to Monticello. These probably twined across country and became the quadruple grandparents of Napa Valley.

For years, America was content with—or intimidated by—California's monopoly. The state employed a hotshot marketing team and convinced the rest of us "Mainlanders" that only ocean breezes and a coastal climate were right. Wrong! Now many states, including my own Minnesota, have great success.

We also produce sneaky authors.

To be honest, all the fore-written has been a subterfuge. For I am a proud vintner, an amateur enologist, a student of the vine.

My kitchen is haven to a tiny brewery. Anyone entering the front hall can verify the permeating aroma.

Space is a problem: With the agility of an arthritic showgirl, I must shimmy over to the table to eat dinner—never daring to disturb the intruding jugs of garnet beauty.

You might wonder how I got to this point. Well, I'll tell you.

I had an epiphany. Or, maybe I read a "How To" book at the beauty shop. Either way, I got hooked.

Reality was not in my favor: The northern climate, the backyard that becomes a lake every spring and my extensive lack of knowledge posed a challenge.

I needed a partner to share the responsibility. That special someone who had a grasp of chemistry so I wouldn't blow up the street where I lived.

Destiny smiled. One day, I just happened to glance out a window and saw my neighbor, the affable doctor. Running to the doorway, I shouted the one phrase no man can resist: "Chocolate cookies, warm from the oven!"

He stepped foot across the threshold. The rest was easy. I convinced him of a rosé-colored future.

Our first executive decision: We decided to do Blueberry Burgundy. Surely such exclusivity would elevate us to celebrity status—if only from the curious.

That July we purchased sixty pounds of little navy nibblers. This ritual is now an annual tradition.

With a surge of joy and dressed in our grubbiest clothing (blueberry stains never come out), we dump the fruit into gigantic tubs. Armed with potato mashers—and a hedonistic attitude—we plunge downward.

Purple splotches and splatters, purple fingers and chins (yes, we do eat a few). Purple grins. Crushed berries begin oozing midnight-hued juices and we start feeling in the pink over the blue.

Sugar, water and a yeast solution are added. The physician medicates with chemicals. Chef here, tests for flavor, while Mr. Hippocratic Oath guards against fungi.

Those first hours are newborn-precarious. I speak to each jug in a soothing tone. I wrap heating pads around their middles to stimulate fermentation. I check their temperature.

Sometimes, I get so tense I take two aspirin. I call the doctor in the morning.

As the mixture ferments, an aroma infiltrates my home. It wafts up the stairway. It bids me sweet dreams and awakens each new day.

Slowly the yeast is activated by the sugar. Then a rapid bubbling occurs. It's so rambunctious at times I fear it will rise like a fluid Frankenstein, assuming a life of its own while the world sleeps.

This happened once. I awakened about five a.m. to strange gurgling noises. Running into the kitchen, I witnessed a twenty-first-century Pompeii. Indigo juice, oozing out of its captive keg, came towards me in a swirling technicolor river.

Foolishly, we had not left enough expansion room at the top of the glass containers. There was no where to go but out.

I called for help. No time for "Good morning. Sorry to disturb you." Only a high-pitched, "Come quickly. Mount Vesuvius is erupting!"

And you thought doctors don't make house calls anymore!

The fizzing and frothing eventually settled down and the process began. Just as it does every year.

It's during this time frame I invite no company. I am captive in a split-level world of booze.

Periodically, I stop and scrutinize, giving each jug a pep talk, always ending with a few supportive words. What works for plants should also help other living organisms. My logic.

After many months it's time to sniff the bouquet, check for clarity, and tipple just a bit. Mind you, this is done strictly for quality assurance. Sometimes, a second glass is required.

Upon reaching an agreement, my accomplice grasps a long plastic tube, inserting one end into the neck of the bottle. The other opening he carefully puts into his mouth so that he can suction the first liquid through.

It's hard to keep a straight face. This skinny curlicue looks like a cross between a musical instrument for Swiss sheepherders and a device for drawing out snakebites.

We fill the bottles proudly and place them in military rows.

I am Captain of the Corks; they must be softened in boiling water. I stand alert at my post, tongs in hand, waiting for each new order.

We then apply the metal covers, sealing each tightly with my yellow hair dryer. Perhaps it's best we don't own a large winery.

The labels "Marvelous Moonshine" are affixed and we sit back and beam.

Another year, another harvest. Our anxious recipients await.

The bottles mature for a year in the cool basement awaiting their showbiz debut the following August.

On the Wednesday of the third week of the eighth month of every year, I put on my lucky shirt: the pink one with lady-bugs embroidered in logical places.

My friend pulls into the driveway and I walk, oh so carefully, towards him carrying the precious container.

With it cradled in my arms, we drive to the Minnesota State Fair to enter the wine contest.

So do over 400 others. All day long, people approach the registration table with offerings of every variety, even corncob and dandelion leaves.

The two of us move deftly towards the women on duty. I instantly become invisible. They see only a handsome doctor holding a bottle of crimson. Their hands stretch out to him. Every word I speak is absorbed by the white wall behind them. Their eyelashes flutter as they wish him success and begin wrapping a paper bag around our contestant. I express my thanks to the air and walk away, hoping they will influence the judges to vote for the tall man in the well-pressed suit. We get to the car, I re-enter my body and we drive home to wait.

Wine is the final judging before the fair opens. On Thursday evening the awards are posted on the Internet. I can't look.

Someone else must gently tell me. Five years we've entered. Four years we've won. Once I delivered the bottle alone. Draw your own conclusions.

The ribbons are beautifully framed and we each get half-a-year to display them. From January to July they hang near my front door so no guest can escape noticing. The other six months, I allude to them in my conversation.

To digress for a moment: The wine area is next to the "seed art" room. Dozens of people, with patience unbeknownst to me, sit tediously with tweezers under hundred-watt bulbs, piecing tiny sesame seeds into the likeness of the Taj Mahal. Others use unpopped corn kernels to resemble Daybreak Over The Rockies.

I was amazed, and suggest when the artists can stand erect again they should visit our ninety-proof products.

Well, I guess my tribute to Bacchus has poured forth.

It feels so good to be a mellow mama. Maybe that's why wine has been around for two thousand years. In moderation, it does nice things for people.

Hopefully, we'll all age as well as fine wine.

Oops—it's five p.m. The cheese and crackers are ready. The sun is setting over the sparkling stemware—and I feel a thirst coming on.

Here's looking at you, kid.

BACK WHEN "CABLE" MEANT A TELEGRAM

Long ago I roamed the Land Before Television, unaware there was more to life than a small brown box called "radio."

My world of entertainment required only a dial. A quick adjustment of the knob brought laughter, romance and suspense, along with static, into the room.

This, I thought, was happiness. This, I know now, was naïve.

Quick flashback to the mid-twentieth-century mind.

We had our radio shows and a newspaper and the back fence. What other forms of communication did a well-informed sophisticate need?

The principle radio was the focal point of the living room. Unlike my desktop model, it boasted spindly legs and a gothic-shaped crown.

Actually, a good-sized piece of furniture, but barely visible as the elders crowded around, leaning in to hear better as FDR reassured the nation during his Fireside Chats.

No one really knew if Roosevelt sat by an actual mantel, but the thought in itself was cozy.

Once in a while, there'd be a picture in *Life* magazine of a seated president somewhere in a room with the backdrop of flickering logs. Today it's known as PR.

Housework was scheduled around the noon Soap Operas. And fortunate school children, home on a mid-day break, swallowed many a peanut butter sandwich serenaded by program music.

Most of the themes were played on the Hammond organ. So many, in fact, I envisioned the soloist wearing special-made shoes to accommodate the constant pedaling. Hard on the instep, you know.

I particularly enjoyed Mr. Kean, Tracer of Lost Persons, whose theme song was "Some Day I'll Find You."

Then there was the story that asked the question: Would a small town girl who married a socialite from Long Island ever find true happiness and use the right fork?

I've worried about her from time to time, but I guess by now they've worked things out.

Best of all was Saturday morning. An added bonus: You didn't have to watch a radio broadcast. A person, if she were so fortunate, could count her bubble gum or stare at the ceiling. All that was needed were ears.

Kids' programs, the granddaddy of Cartoon Network, ran until noon. During station breaks I'd grab snacks that didn't disclose crumbs, returning to my hideout under the covers. Joy was spelled PHILCO.

Sunday nights, all across the Midwest, families would sit down to dinner with famous personalities, great wits who set the bar for today's late-night talent.

I was careful to sip my tomato soup quietly, not to annoy my brother (thereby avoiding a kick under the table). Crackers could only be crunched during commercials.

One day my complacency was interrupted by two men carrying an enormous carton.

My life changed with a doorbell.

"Where do you want it, Mister?" they asked my father.

It went into the den. The rest of us followed.

This "thing" became uncrated and stood there glaring at me defiantly. I glared back, awestruck.

My dad, as the patriarch in these situations, uttered the initial sentence. "I bought you something new—a television set."

Of course I'd heard about this phenomenon in science class but here, infiltrating my home, an intruder had come to live among us.

"Turn it on," was sentence two.

We did. A geometric design, soon to be termed a "Test Pattern," emerged. And stayed on eighteen hours a day. Someone forgot to tell the networks to create programs.

At midnight the Test Pattern would be replaced by the American flag waving to the national anthem. And then, all would go black until yesterday became tomorrow.

It was less than fascinating. I couldn't wait to resume my Saturday radio mornings complete with my stash of Caramel Milk Duds.

We kept the Newcomer dusted, we put a green plant on top, and we went about our lives.

Eventually, a lucrative sponsor woke the sleeping CBS and Sunday-night programming appeared.

Ours was the new box on the block. And word got out.

The neighbor families made a weekly vigil to our front hall. Careful to wipe their feet. Taking no chances ensuing invites would be negated.

Over fifteen and you got a chair. All others crowded the rug.

The guest of honor that evening turned the "on" knob. To us it equaled the champagne launching of a maiden voyage.

We heard and saw images simultaneously. Both an audio and visual performance.

What progress the world had made since candles!

Kraft Playhouse enacted a drama, comic Milton Berle did a one-hour shtick. All in breath-taking black and white, with a hint of gray.

Everyone speculated how color could possibly be added; no, that was too over-the-top for this decade.

Somewhere between curtain calls and slapstick my father would appear among us wearing a vendor's hat, much like those worn at a baseball game. Over each shoulder was a makeshift strap supporting a large protruding box filled with Crackerjacks, Butterfinger bars and apples. During the breaks he'd announce the menu and weave among the guests filling requests.

As the last canned applause diminished, the picture faded and old reliable Test Pattern reappeared.

The room was emptied and so were the wastebaskets.

The boat-shaped hat was placed on a shelf, its partner snack box nearby.

Another Sunday night concluded. Tomorrow began a whole week of radio shows. And those of us who were loyal, listened, imagining what we didn't see.

Whatever became of the lost art of sound effects? All those gainfully employed wizards of wind blowing and footsteps down a cobblestone path. I suppose they went into the same unemployment line as street car conductors and typewriter repairmen.

Today it's all about quick communication squeezed into small electronics.

As an example, the Palm Pilot. My initial comprehension was Northwest Airlines must have submitted one of their own to shrinking vapors and now, poor chap, fits in the size of an open hand.

How disastrous for his family. Reminds me of P. T. Barnum's marketing of Tom Thumb.

In truth, it's merely a misnomer—a term for the less imaginative.

TV, as it came to be known, is the Grande Dame of countless enterprises and has played a game with the English language.

A "channel" once referred to the waterway between England and France. "Remote" meant a distance greater than one hundred miles. "Fax" was information needed for a report. "Online" showed you could color within the spaces. "Software" was one hundred percent cotton and "website" indicated you should dust more often.

Point proven.

With a group effort, very bright people collaborated on a brainchild and gave so many, in one invention, education and pleasure and countless jobs.

Sure it's been exploited, but every good product has.

I'm not judging. Just appreciating genius.

We still use radios while driving to work and to keep us company in the back of the shop. But they've had to acquiesce to cutting-edge advancement. As it should be.

Those annoying test patterns are part of history and so is the resulting eye strain.

The wonderful paradox: While technology advances, people remain constant.

Neighbors get together because they like each other, hat shops are open for business, and families still eat tomato soup on Sunday nights.

Some things cannot be improved on.

Red, White and Sometimes Blue

I can lip-sync the national anthem as well as anyone in the ballpark. But when I fake it, I'm sincere.

It's part of my job profile.

I was born on the Fourth of July, and with that certificate issued at city hall comes a psychological list of obligations.

Some a nuisance, many an honor.

Initially, I'm told, the attending hospital staff tried to convince my parents to name me "Glory." Several decades later this would result in "Old Glory."

Fortunately, the memory of an obscure relative saved me and I became the female derivative of Morris.

As each birthday occurred, an observation did not. I remained oblivious to historical dates and assumed all the fuss and fanfare was only for me.

Father stayed home from work for the explicit purpose of taking me on a pony ride. Those explosive fireworks boldly proclaimed to the moon and stars that a child toddled beneath them.

I clung to sweet naïveté. Never once asking the question I didn't want answered.

Eventually, I was forced to confront the truth: The entire country stayed home. Not necessarily to ride a horse, but, at the very least, to have a picnic which was ceremoniously concluded by a shower of sparklers meant to amuse those onlookers whose dinner of bratwurst and sauerkraut did not produce heartburn (thus forcing them to leave early.)

I made my peace with the holiday. My piece of cake, however, was an annual frustration.

Every self-respecting bakery would decorate only in red, white and blue. How I hungered for pink and green. It never happened. I was always stuck with sapphire-colored frosting that stained mouths an odd hue.

Hours after, guests at my party appeared to be experiencing a chill in July. In truth, it was the lingering icing that turned their lips blue.

Those of us born on the "Fourth" have fifty stars to bear. We accept with grace and aplomb the endless wisecracks, "So, you started life with a bang" or "You're a red-hot baby," ad infinitum.

We must endure this every time a questionnaire or résumé is filled out.

We handle the paper gingerly, knowing, inevitably, what we will hear. We're expected to laugh. And we do, on the outside.

As the millennium year approached, Philadelphia wanted to re-enact the birth of America.

An advertisement went out on all media searching for everybody in my category. One person representing each of the past hundred years would be selected to drive in a parade heralding the gala.

I submitted a nice picture of myself toasting a make-believe celebration with a glass of invisible liquid, and enclosed the qualifying credentials.

The mail-carrier and I bonded waiting together for an invitation.

None came.

I later learned I was trumped by identical triplets and a gentleman whose dog also shared the day.

Oh well, it turned out there was a hot spell in the East, so who would've wanted to ride in an open car, anyhow?

Or, perhaps I looked so young for my age the judges disqualified me. No response, please.

In tribute to my country, I decorated the den in patriotic colors. Everyone who enters comments before reclining on the red chaise. Maybe they're just startled by a couch usually seen only on the stage of a Tennessee Williams play.

And, speaking of theater, I catch the classic movie "Yankee Doodle Dandy" occasionally. I'll never tire of watching James Cagney tip-tapping his metal heels as he rhythmically struts across a vaudevillian stage, boasting he's the nephew of Uncle Sam. Under that supposition I qualify as niece to a hypothetical uncle who passed on without leaving me anything in his will.

But, I have inherited a pride of ownership; sharing the day with the Continental Congress and Louis Armstrong.

My driver's license is a valid testimonial.

Even though I lied about my weight.

Innovative Inventions

If necessity is the mother of invention, my brainchildren must surely be orphans. I admit I've never once awakened in the night and shouted "Eureka! I've contributed to mankind."

My humble ideas clearly are not going to alter history, compared to the wheel and white bread, but I do have a list of unique donations to offer this world.

Take, for example, the Electric Coat. In all actuality, an electric blanket with arms.

Living in a northern climate, this would be a frugal investment in any wardrobe. One garment, four seasons.

A stylish wrap, complete with patch pockets and a removable hood.

"Yes," you agree. "But wouldn't the wearer require a lengthy extension cord attached to an electrical outlet?"

"No," I'd reply. "It would be battery powered."

Included in the purchase price, I'd throw in long-lasting Energizers to get you started. Limited assembly required.

Consider the advantage: Instead of assorted toppers and cumbersome parkas, one coat with an adjustable temperature control (carried in the convenient patch pockets) would do the job.

Available in stylish colors with contrasting collar and cuffs. It would save on closet space, too. No need to store out-of-season garments, because—you're catching on—this little number would be year 'round.

The only part I haven't figured out is how not to get slightly electrocuted if caught in a sudden downpour.

The wearer, therefore, would need to frequently glance upward, and perhaps take a crash course in meteorology.

Basic rule: Learn to anticipate and be cognizant of covered doorways.

After a while, this behavior would become routine and the Electric Coat will be your fondest possession.

I couldn't restrict you to outer garments only.

I've designed shoes, as well. Again, geographically influenced—made for snow and ice—but also adaptable for sun and surf.

Indoor-outdoor, all-season golf shoes. Perfect even for those of you who think a birdie has wings.

Suitable for all ages, with built-in arch supports optional and, of course, a handsome match to the aforementioned coat.

The big difference here is the sole. My design would have golf-like cleats. This would enable the wearer to safely walk on slippery surfaces, up steep hills, and along wet, sandy beaches.

They'd be a big seller in San Francisco, not to mention South Beach.

Available in three heel heights and a weather-proof finish.

The one problem is entering the house. Each pair would include a bag of plugs to cover the shoe bottoms so holes from the soles would not penetrate carpeting.

Either that, or you could just kick them off at the door.

A set of cozy slippers would accompany each sale. Gratis.

Don't thank me.

It's my pleasure.

In any word-association, shoes are matched with socks—my next quest.

Unbeknownst to the human mind, there must be a land to which lost socks wander.

Not found on any map or listed in the National Geographic Index, this hideaway is beyond our comprehension.

A sort of Sock Shangri-la.

Millions, even billions, of footwear belonging to everyone who's ever been on Earth, go there to rest, and to avoid feet. In a sense, it's mutiny; they will never be put on again.

What could lure them back? My remote-control "Sock Sleuth," developed for just such a challenge.

I have not yet, at this writing, spoken to a manufacturer. But this would be my sales pitch:

A package of twenty-four tiny batteries, similar to those used in hearing aids, would be encapsulated in a waterproof cloth. These "receivers" would then be attached with fabric glue to the ribbing of each sock (enough for one-dozen pair, so you needn't do laundry too often.)

Press the remote control, listen for the signal—and uncover their hideout.

When not in use, put the control back in its base to re-charge—much like an electric toothbrush.

The "Sleuth" could locate strays that fell behind the washer, were left in the suitcase since last August or are keeping dust bunnies company under the bed. There's just no limit.

Many a duffel bag will take on a sweet new fragrance after my invention is used.

Business associates will not notice the ankle gizmos because they'll blend with every outfit: Brown on one side, reversing to black. White would be introduced after Memorial Day. This will be nice for Jocks, too. They'll never know de-feet (forgive the pun.)

A final hard sell. Thanks to the "Sleuth" you'll be able to:

1. Put your feet up on the desk,

2. Flippantly kick off your shoes when confronted with white carpeting, and

3. Finally enjoy the ambience of a Japanese restaurant.

Look down, you'll hold your head up proudly. There's something beautiful touching the floor: Two socks that match.

Let's hear it for confidence.

From feet to hands, the search continues.

According to the Fashion Police, glitzy accessories are the ticket. My adult-designed clips for gloves and ski mittens provide security and style simultaneously.

Somewhere, this side of the Alps, there must be a mountain-sized pile of single gloves accumulated over years of losing them one-at-a-time.

I myself have been a generous contributor to this eminence.

Just when I work the glove fingers enough to bend with mine, the honeymoon is over, and one waves "good-bye."

Whether it falls from a pocket, is dropped at the checkout counter, or becomes a surrogate bone for Fido, the dumb thing disappears.

It's so awkward wearing a glove on one hand and keeping the other inside a fastened coat, somewhat like Napoleon. It's hard to drive a car that way, too. Remember, Bonaparte rode a horse.

You need my clips.

Made from simulated Austrian crystal, this stunning jewelry would hinge on one side of the coat sleeve, while the other attaches to the glove edge.

Removable and, if made in quantity, quite reasonably priced. A unisex style could also be designed in lamb leather.

The clips would be acceptable for all age groups and enjoyed until that day the inevitable happens.

You lose one.

C'est la vie.

Now that fingers and toes have been addressed, I will describe my line of disposable clothing: Knock-off Armani's made from heavy-duty paper. This is my answer to a laundry-free life; and don't even mention ironing.

Wear it to the party, throw it out the morning after.

Inexpensive and perfectly safe since smoking is banned in most public places.

Just watch the car doors and candlelight dinners.

For my next endeavor, I present to you the potentially famous "Choose-a-Juice."

Actually, I wrote to a large manufacturer about this. I even got a reply. It was "No."

Not because it was an absurd idea. They informed me they'd already thought of it themselves.

I've had the squeeze put on me enough to know they wanted to eliminate me from their grandiose plans—when they've canned their first million.

Oh well, I've got the blue print memorized. This is how it would work: Everyone in the family wants something different to sip. Instead of purchasing several cumbersome containers, my "Choose-a-Juice" would be a convenient six-pack of various flavors. Easy to grasp in the store and simple to store at home.

With pull-off tops to grab instead of reaching for shameful candy, you'd get a medically approved, convenient snack, and make me rich, too.

I would perform acts of kindness with the money.

Let's stay on food and I will continue with another brilliant conception that will never hit the market—my "Cone Cuff."

Americans eat gallons of ice cream annually. Every Fourth of July I see statistics on the Food Network substantiating this claim.

Trouble is, the higher the butterfat content, the faster the melting point.

I've never admitted this before, but if I'm going to indulge, it's got to be the good stuff—not whipped air.

Therefore, I'm in a perpetual dilemma; I can't lick fast enough. Especially with a talkative group. Can a true aficionado spare one minute to converse—and risk a "drip" deadline?

I don't think so.

We've all been there on a summer afternoon.

My solution: The merchant, upon scooping a double-dipper into a waffle cone, would then secure a paper cuff around the round.

This "catcher" curves slightly upward enabling the consumer to discreetly ingest accumulated slush.

Not only is this a delicious alternative, but it also insures no one returns to the office wearing a pink peppermint monogram.

One final food fancy: I need a round spreader (not to be confused with "I'm round and spreading.")

You do too.

Imagine a small implement for putting butter, jam and everything else on a circled surface.

I can't figure out why generations of intelligent people have wrestled with long, skinny tools when applying toppings on squat little scones.

Yes, there are ornate-handled cocktail spreaders to use after 5 p.m. and my kitchen drawer houses a variety of odd-shaped utensils. But what the world needs today is a genuine Fat Knife.

One wide enough to encompass the circumference of a Florida onion roll.

We've delved into the universe, why then, should this be so difficult?

I'm tired of making four trips in and out of the cream cheese to plaster the outer dimensions of lunch.

One swoop and it's covered, and so is this subject.

Well, there you have it—my compilation of devious, if not dubious, devices.

Feel free to patent any of them.

But just remember my favorite words: You heard it here first.

Life Savers

Every night when I am sleeping, a troop of gnomes from an uncharted galaxy enter my home.

These little fellows stealthily deposit paraphernalia from all over the world into closets and bureau drawers.

An executive committee gets the choice jobs: Junking up my desk and dining room table. When I go to bed, I could testify under oath that those two pieces of furniture have wooden surfaces. Come morning there's nothing to be seen but massive clutter.

No cherrywood found here, Your Honor.

I can't comprehend this metamorphosis.

Where does the mess come from? Me, I'm as neat and tidy as person needs to be.

Why, then, is my home a research project?

I'm becoming convinced there are secret entries to my house. I remember the contractor had a slippery handshake.

Or, perhaps as a child, I watched too many mystery matinees.

The fumbling detective, attempting to avoid a suit of clanging armor, accidentally leans against a bookcase in the isolated mansion. With shocking surprise (reinforced by an organ vibrato on the sound track), the wall gives way to a dark—and, we assume, musty—tunnel.

Foolheartedly, the Investigator, along with a Man of Science, declare their intentions: They will enter the black unknown and, therefore, find the good-looking ingénue who will, out of sheer gratitude, fall in love with either or both of them.

Thereby ending the movie and the popcorn, if carefully paced, concurrently.

The truth: Like so many others, I have a tendency to save. It's not that I'm conscious of this habit, but I just don't want to part with something that someday could evolve into a treasure on eBay.

I hold on—and on.

A magazine is delivered. I must find time to read. Next week certainly. Meanwhile, there might be a fifty-cents-off coupon on one page and words of advice to memorize on another. No discarding that jewel.

Papers to contemplate are together in a folder. Insurance info and financial reports require an alert mind. One of these days, I'm going to get up at five a.m. and study each paragraph. I'll sort the superfluous and try to find my shredder.

Receipts, those crumpled little papers pinched together in my oversized paperclip, must be saved just in case.

Not only could a sweater sleeve unravel, but a friend might want to return (hard to believe) her birthday gift—the 8 x 10 picture of four dogs playing poker on a black velvet background. I'll have a sales slip ready.

No, I won't be hurt. But, next year, she'll get a gift certificate.

The restaurant take-out menus are stacked on the far left. They're only useful for unexpected company, and I'd rather whip up Spanish omelets for a crowd.

Business cards of plumbers used two years ago and address books filled with relatives who have long since moved are items I must sort through on a quiet Sunday. Then we'll part ways.

My buried treasures are truly encapsulated in the deepest desk drawers. Pictures of "stick" mothers with curly dark hair and smiley faces are yellowed and crinkled with years. But, they remain beautiful.

A timeless Valentine—the affirmation of love—my umbrella for every rainy day I encounter.

They must stay just where they are. Next to the desk is my bookcase. Filled with out-of-print volumes. Not necessarily important classics. Many small works by authors forgotten after a first printing.

Of course, there are shelves of cookbooks. Dozens filled with recipes I hesitate to prepare: Deep-fried anything topped with a cream sauce, and desserts never to be mentioned at a cardiologists' convention. A library of gastronomical good ol' days.

My eyes sweep across the rooms, each holding reminders of my vacations—or someone else's.

I remember when I saw the hand-carved donkey, scattered among all the other souvenirs at an open-air market. I bartered in a foreign language for it—each of us thinking we got a good buy.

I remember the painting, barely dry, I bought right off the easel in Montmartre. The artist thanked me too profusely as he rolled up the canvas. It cracked apart in my suitcase. I'd like to think he didn't know that would happen.

It's down in the basement storeroom. I can't throw it out.

Oh, that storeroom—and the trunk filled with yearbooks, and all the faces that didn't yet require airbrushing. I saved the programs, too—from those exciting musical shows with a one-weekend run.

A sentimental journey includes a walk up the stairs. Welcome to Collectors Anonymous.

But how did it all get here? And who sent it? And why is it residing in my house?

Tucked in a cupboard is a small blue pitcher with a picture. Shirley Temple, half rubbed off, smiles coquettishly as her curls bounce about. The other side of her head has been hopelessly lost due to an over-zealous kitchen towel.

I use it only to serve maple syrup, its sweetness synonymous with her reputation.

On the same shelf are my salt and peppers sculpted with ancient Greek faces. I found them at Disneyland. Can you imagine two matched pairs on mark-down?

They'll never see a yard sale. Nor will my salad bowl shaped like the Coliseum. The serving utensils resemble Julius and Mrs. Caesar.

I vividly recall purchasing these items. The clerk's hands trembled with excitement as he clutched my check. Before I left the store I overheard him exclaiming into his cell phone, "Whoopee, honey, we're going out to dinner tonight. I unloaded the albatross!"

I've always wondered if I inspired that reaction.

On the buffet sits a hand-painted tea set missing one cup, watched over by a porcelain cowboy with six fingers on his left hand. (The mold must have been faulty.) So many one-of-a-kinds discovered at a flea market. Or channel-surfing the television shopping networks.

Wherever the origin, they're part of the family now.

Over the fireplace hangs a visual anthology of pastries detailing the evolution of pies, muffins and cakes.

A print-order of one. And it's mine.

There are gifts from people important enough to share my table, whose laughter warmed my dreams that night.

Step into my doorway. You'll know what I'm all about.

Each possession explains me, just as your home gives others the same message.

I will never be featured in *Décor to Adore* monthly, and how I acquired all this loot is absolutely baffling.

I'd like to blame it on an inter-planetary invasion—but I truly think it's just plain me.

I'll start cleaning out one corner of one room tomorrow.

You can trust me. As much as the guy who said he could eat one potato chip.

A SHORT SPORT REPORT

I'm one of the guys at a Super Bowl party, happily sitting among the bottles of beer while strange words like "conversion" and "touchback" emanate from the mouth attached to my face. I holler constructive criticism to the coach who perpetually fails to take my advice.

So let 'em be down two field goals, I warned him.

Call me, for three hours on a Sunday, a Regular Fellow. Football is my game and I'm in it with the best of them.

How this happened to someone who's never even had athlete's foot cannot be explained.

I do admire purple (as in Vikings) and the massive tattooed arms of the linebackers. I imagine cooking for them, their biceps flexing as they reach for my sliced brisket in mushroom gravy. Third helpings available.

Perhaps the rough 'n' tumble faction of me screams to emerge from pink ruffles. Perhaps a gladiator mentality has been secreted away in a past life. Who knows?

I look over. The other women chat together in hushed voices respectful of the drama across the room. Occasionally one will inquire, "What's the score?" I recite numerals with an edge of arrogance. I know. I've been watching.

I can also tell immediately which quarterback threw the ball because he's in a sharper color combination than the opposing team.

I'm aware, too, why the players wear black smudges under their eyes—much like mascara after a good cry.

But I cannot tell you how their outfits stay so clean throughout a long season.

Does the team have new jerseys every game? Is there a salary cap for the crew who wash clothes?

What a soap commercial that could be: "Use our product. Kick the astro out of your laundry."

I'm fascinated, too, with those small yellow scarves the referees keep throwing onto the field. How quaint to play Drop the Handkerchief as in olden days. Seems to me the Ref should just yell "Stop playing—you goofed." But that would be too simple.

Of course I dread seeing anyone get punched and fall down. I worry for their mothers.

I've noticed some of my buddies subtly move over to another sofa. It's certainly not because I ask so many insightful questions. I think they just want to be closer to the Cheetos.

The Super Bowl only concludes many months of loyal viewing. I stop whatever I'm doing on every autumnal Sunday so I can be with my club. They'll never appreciate such devotion—or know how I struggle to stay awake during the third quarter (something in the air seems to weigh down my eyelids).

I've come late to more than one Sunday night potluck supper just so I could see the winners throw a bucket of water over their coach—or watch the battle of overtime. (I dream of owning an anti-anxiety Rx concession).

Being a pigskin groupie is an anomaly for a consistently non-sports existence.

I've tried and failed at almost every athletic endeavor, all the way back to junior high school gym class.

Her name was Miss Kidd. She should have been called "Miss Nomer" because she wasn't kidding about insisting I perform a somersault.

Let me put it this way: I was born with a congenital apprehension about rolling into a ball and taking my feet off solid flooring. There's just something unnatural about that and I wanted no part of it. My parents were called to school but no amount of persuasion or bribes stirred me. I stood my ground. Literally.

My nemesis was a short square phys ed. teacher who dressed in a grey pinstriped suit from September until June. Hopefully, she owned several identical ensembles. But it didn't really matter because I avoided her with polished deftness.

Her only accessory was a tarnished whistle attached to a plastic chain, which I assumed she wove for herself back in her camping days.

When she blew a flat high "C" on that tooter, we girls were to form into a long line for tumbling.

Each participant approached the mat gleefully with a running start. Giggling with success, and praise from teacher, she'd then rejoin the formation for another wonderful go 'round.

I had to think quickly. Two more classmates and then me.

I stepped out of line to re-strengthen my tennis ties. Amazingly, the girl behind me moved forward. I gazed up at the ceiling and said, "Thank You."

I slid to the back of the line and kept on sliding until, mercifully, the bell sounded. I had chanced upon a technique to help me through the semester.

At the conclusion I received a passing grade. No, I didn't improve. The old Kidd just couldn't look at me in line any longer.

Compliment returned: To this day I have never worn, nor have I ever purchased, anything resembling grey pinstripes.

My agility continued to be a non-asset.

Upon entering tenth grade I was informed that, besides dissecting a frog in science class, there was a mandatory Wednesday swim class, which I assure you was no romp on the beach.

The issued blue suits were made from a fabric unknown in the Garment District. Undoubtedly, they were government surplus. Besides that, each one had holes in unbecoming places. Previous inhabitants must have strained strategic seams.

What to do? I couldn't slip to the end of the line because there was no line. We were all to plunge in together.

I did know how to stay afloat. But the over-chlorinated pool affected my nasal passages. Besides, the suit itched and the rubber cap left a strange scalloped design on my forehead most of the afternoon.

How did this end?

Well, drawing on my inner strength to be a good sport, I dog-paddled around until I heard the beautiful, "Everybody out of the water." Having positioned myself by the edge for the final ten minutes of class, I, naturally, was first one up and over.

Wasn't easy. The swimsuits absorbed water. Each retaining several pounds after a dunking, increasing their bulk and leaving a residue of puddles as thundering thong-footed bluebirds overtook the girls' locker room.

It's a wonder any of us were asked to marry.

The decades progressed; my athletic dexterity did not.

Everyone was playing tennis. It didn't look too difficult to hammer a little ball across a large net. I got a snappy outfit and an instructor. In that order. Funny though, he only lasted two lessons and then told me he was moving out of town—right after I asked him what all the white lines meant.

Regardless, I took great pleasure in owning those socks with the cute colored balls in the back. I'd deliberately wear them to an upscale grocery store. Everyone between potatoes and tomatoes, I imagined, was looking with respect and wondering which tournament I'd just won.

No one ever commented. But I could feel their eyes.

The years—and my futile attempts—continued.

I tried golf. But nobody was ever available to play. Coincidentally, each potential partner had just made plans ten minutes before I called.

I was down to croquet. But it was too hard on the backyard.

What was left for me?

I had managed to mobilize myself throughout life by putting one foot in front of the other. So I settled on simply walking. There's something so reassuring about the sound of lapping waves, the reflection of the sky on the water. It speaks of calm. Finally, I discovered my sport—and joy.

To all of you non-athletes, don't apologize. Spectators are important and I'm not just referring to those black and white shoes worn during the summer.

Our support and applause are needed by all these brawny participants who like to sweat.

We'll watch from a hammock.

COUNTER INTELLIGENCE

There may be no business like show business—but nothing is finer than dinner at a diner.

Anyplace, USA, restaurants happily nurture us.

A place to meet and eat—and treat ourselves to a few hours of the Good Life. By any name, "Gastric Gerties" to "La Maison d'Expense Account," an eatery is the base of our sociability. Hardly a day goes by when we don't go to a fast-food counter, a coffeehouse or neighborhood grill. They're all inviting.

Did you ever stop, in the midst of your cappuccino, to appreciate how all this began?

Picture, please, a huge open hearth with a group of the wig and cloak boys settled around, each swirling their ale-filled pewter mugs. In the background, the innkeeper ladles their favorite peanut soup and carves whatever was caught that afternoon to serve with it.

Happily, we no longer need to brave the woods to shoot supper. Now all we shoot is the "breeze"—and that comes quite easily to most of us.

Our Founding Fathers frequented many such establishments.

Possibly because our Founding Mothers objected to spending their days churning and, perhaps, burning. Their goose was cooked—and so was the chance of eating at home.

So there they sat, in their uncomfortable wooden chairs, toasting a new nation—and marveling at the byproducts of corn and rye.

This premise remains. We get together in jovial surroundings, to chat over drinks and dinner.

The conversation is still the same. We gripe about heavy taxation and problems across The Pond.

America was founded on democracy—and really good taverns, the latter substantiating the former.

Along with waistcoats, the country expanded. Eventually, covered wagons surged westward, filled with settlers desperately fighting the heat and desert dryness. Something had to be done quickly to appease their thirst. Enterprising frontiersmen simply added an "O" to the genteel "salons" of the East and made it their own. The "saloon" swung open its door to the tired, the parched. Everyone re-hydrated and some even struck gold.

Back in Dodge City, the bartenders wanted to increase sales so they introduced a free lunch of particularly salty foods. Suds soared.

To complete the ambience, the proprietor added a few decks of marked cards – and some women referred to as "Tarts"— who were, in no way, accomplished bakers. Although they often served as dessert.

Enough of my extensive historical data. Let's talk about today.

Restaurants are such a major part of our lifestyle that you can't even walk past a newsstand without noticing a proud chef—flushed from standing over a simmering soup kettle— imprinted on a magazine cover. His vanilla hat sits so tall that headlines must be lettered across the pleated top. The smiling eyes, the chubby chinline entice us to experience an art form. And bring a Visa card.

We're entranced and make a reservation. But so do a hundred others. We arrive to meet them all at the coat check.

The maître d' recites his well-rehearsed spiel about running late because other guests are lingering.

We wait at the bar. There're peanuts there. With refills. Only Nostradamus could predict when our table will be ready.

When we're finally seated, the basket of bread is an extra charge. So is water. Inevitably, the person before us orders the last House Special. I enter the realm of crabby, driven to toss four sugar packets into my purse. Revenge is sweet.

The paper-faced chef who lured us here must have slipped out by the back exit. The food is good, but by ten p.m., so is a can of soup at home. That brings up another point.

Why do people go out to eat "home cooking"?

There's no logic, so it must be all about nostalgia, remembering warm apple pie and Mom in an idealized painting by Norman Rockwell. A canvas of a kitchen table laden with pot roast. Institute of Fine Arts quality.

Dining out has even developed into reality TV—showing restaurateurs fidgeting and fighting with backers about opening the new hotspot in town.

Watch next week: Will the naugahyde barstools be delivered on time? Can soaring budgets and egos be controlled? Will the sous chef accidentally set a fire in the rotisserie? Personalities flare—and so do the kabobs.

All these questions will never be resolved because the thirteen-week series ends. It's not my kind of place, anyhow. In the meantime, I'll open another can of soup. Help yourself to chicken noodle.

It's gratifying for diverse nationalities and ethnic groups to display their cuisine. I get to tickle my taste buds; they perpetuate a heritage and pay the mortgage, too.

Countries and cultures most of us never encounter can be savored at the counter.

It amazes me how everything different is really the same: Ravioli becomes wonton, strudel transforms into spring rolls and pâté is still chopped liver.

You can scarcely enter a building without finding an alcove to dine. Offices have captive employees, department stores provide shoppers with quick energy to continue purchasing and, of course, hotels perpetuate those lengthening guest tabs.

Even patrons of the arts are offered dinner before theater. I fantasize opening such an attraction. I'll name it "Chew on an Aisle."

Yes, I'm aware that excludes the center row crowd. But I can't cater to the entire auditorium. Yet.

Have you noticed the most popular restaurants are the noisiest? I hear it's all about emulating chic Manhattan.

Maybe New Yorkers have a secret method: They e-mail topics of interest to each other two hours before meeting. Then, with designated signals, they just nod appropriately.

Conversation may be old-fashioned. But so am I. I enjoy listening to a friend. That is, if I can find her in a large gathering.

I wish I had a plat du jour for every time I don't connect at the right entrance or correct place.

We're alert people. Why, then, is it so difficult to meet in front of—not behind—the potted palm? And who gave permission to have two doors into the same café?

Booths should never be as high as office modules. Is it my fault if I arrive early because my feet hurt and I take a table? I don't think so. I still should be able to gaze out across the room, and the hostess should remember to tell my companion a sweet-faced woman is waiting.

Doesn't happen. I must either put back on those miserable but stunning shoes or wave my arms broadly—like a flabby cheerleader.

No wonder I need a glass of wine before lunch.

How heartwarming that most of us open our homes to a lonely dog, as verified by the quantity of doggie bags packed at the table. I must be truthful. My pet no longer resides with me. But I've eaten the contents of many such-marked sacks in his memory. I know you share the same sentiment.

And speaking of emotions, I cannot conclude my dissertation on eateries without including my waitperson, Debbie, who will be serving me all evening. I realize management instructed her to build a relationship. Tipping is calculated on customer service and I want the best for her. But we're not going to develop a lasting relationship. I'm a one-night stand, honey.

Please, Deborah, just bring the food hot and cool yourself down.

What would we all do without a good place to dine? The bowling alley's too loud, the park's not safe after dark and you have to whisper in the library.

Expensive or crowded, our restaurants give us pleasure— and serve us well.

Take notice, the first four letters spell REST. We could all use more of that.

SMALLER IS BETTER

Most of my life, I've thought the best three words in the English language were *I Love You*. While everyone agrees a person cannot hear this too often, I've come to realize there are many other three-word sentences that can enhance a life.

I grabbed a notebook, put my feet up, and just off the top of my head, began a list:

My favorite phrase is *Let It Go*. Three single syllables that could put the antacid business into Chapter 11. Words important enough to be ingrained on every pair of shoes so the inhabitant could glance down, as needed, throughout the day.

During a meeting, when no one agrees with your point of view, quickly drop your pen under the table. Others will assume you're searching. We know better; you're chanting your Italian leather loafers. Arise refreshed.

And if, while driving down the street, someone swerves in front of you with verbal instructions about your anatomy, just glance at your pedal foot.

Let It Go helps relationships, too. When remarks cut more than the air, the motto on your sneakers will help you jog away to the land of *Keep Your Cool*. A cousin to the shoe sage.

This one is oh so impressive, from the board room to the just plain bored. "Keeping cool" does not refer to a tall lemonade, linen jackets that don't look slept-in, or hair that won't frizz up in humidity. "Cool" means dignity under fire, composure when the tornado inside you is raging to break loose.

All of which leads to *Hang In There*. Although it sounds plausible, this doesn't refer to a substance for strengthening fingernails. It does, however, fortify internally and is individually manufactured under the generic title "courage."

See, I told you. Little sentences. Big Ideas.

Another winner is *I'll Diet Tomorrow*. Exclaimed frequently with great sincerity, this trio is a total paradox to *Bake Until Golden*, my personal favorite for professional reasons.

The Battery's Dead is particularly popular at Christmas time among young children who repeat it loudly during the football game. This sentence is generally followed by bellowing and a plea to find a convenience store that stays open on a holiday evening.

Home Sweet Home is a natural follow-up to the aforementioned. So is *Some Assembly Required*, although this much-dreaded tagline applies all year 'round. You can assume any item in a box larger than 8½" x 11" will require reading glasses and a Phillips screwdriver. If necessary, re-read *Keep Your Cool*.

In The Beginning when we were all gullible youths, the words *I'll Call You* were easily accepted. As we matured, the sparkle dust tarnished and we now interpret the word "Earnest" as merely a male proper noun.

Many a hopeful entertainer has edged her way to the wings hearing the *Don't Call Me, I'll Call You* heart-sinker.

During interviews or at a party *I'll Call You* concludes before the qualifying words *Sometime This Century*.

However, you must always *Call Your Mother*. Especially if you've recently had a cold. She needs reassurance you're not as nasal.

Now with e-mail, faxes and voice mail, it's so easy to communicate you no longer can use the excuse "you must have been taking a bath and didn't hear the phone."

Take my advice or you'll be saying *Please Forgive Me.*

A favorite of every athletic coach, piano teacher and all parents who ever lived is *Do Your Best*. There is not a sliding scale for this one. No one ever uttered *Try For Mediocrity*.

Doing one's best is initially heard when taking baby steps. It shadows a student all through school to a first job résumé. The sun doesn't go down without that criterion lurking everywhere. It haunts us. It taunts us.

I vote that once in a while we should all have a chance to screw up. It would feel good.

Do Not Disturb. This sign on a hotel door means the room will remain cluttered. Someone should print a sign for foreheads. In small print it would read, "My thoughts are delightfully dancing. Please do not enter. I do not wish to be tidied up."

Because I want to *Celebrate The Ordinary,* with moments to watch the kindergarten class holding onto a rope chain as they're carefully escorted down the street, a little time to savor a peppermint or leaf through a book.

Each day is extraordinary because we own it for just a brief while—and *Money Isn't Everything.*

Considering I make pastries, you'd assume *Spread the Sweetness* refers to warm peach pie á la mode. It does. Only more so. Throw a little sugar around and you've got a better chance of living *Happily Ever After.*

Add to that *I'll Take Chocolate* and *This Chapter's Finished.*

I'll Be Seeing You…

Tonight I will not vacuum. In fact, I am faced with an option: To donate my Hoover upright and take a tax deduction, or spend the next hour bending from the waist.

My carpeting is completely covered with strange segments of paper. Blue shag barely visible under a blanket of "Notes to Self."

Peering across—much like a High Priestess—I survey not my subjects but my subject matter: Thousands of black scrawlings usually referred to as "Handwriting."

In my case, thousands of notations. My personal hieroglyphics.

Over more hours than you want to hear about, I've played with this manuscript. Coaxing words into cohesive sentences, teasing each line into ideas to explore or, perhaps, ignore. Progressing to Plan B.

My pens have scattered and fallen, plastic warriors, only a click away from doing battle with clichés.

I sincerely believe my right index finger will be permanently indented from clutching the slender cylinders. As my Aunt Rose would have said, "I have writer's cramps."

Why don't I use a computer? Because composing long-hand immerses me into my art; I need a tactile connection.

Slowly stretching myself vertical, the crunchy papers feel almost silken under my bare wiggly toes.

The noisy footsteps keep no secrets, announcing my journey—our journey together—through each page.

Thank you for allowing me to tickle your imagination—and travel with you to a place where sweet memories are made.

Some day we'll meet again—Volume Two, Page One.

Margie

RECIPES

1. *Tomato Soup to Sip Softly* *100*

2. *Ice Cream to Eat in a Dish at Home* *101*

3. *Bargaining Brownies* *103*

4. *Saturday Morning Snacks to Hide for Yourself.*
   a. Pecan Crunchies *104*
   b. Cracker Snackers *105*

5. *Somersault Sweeties* *106*

6. *Tarts. No Explanation Necessary.*
   a. Apple & Apricot Tart *107*
   b. Pear Tart with Almond Cream *109*

TOMATO SOUP TO SIP SOFTLY

SERVES 6

4 tablespoons butter

2 carrots, sliced thin

2 celery stalks, sliced thin

2 onions, sliced thin

2 tablespoons flour

2 pounds canned whole tomatoes in thick puree

2 cups water

3 cups rich beef broth

1 teaspoon honey

1 teaspoon lemon pepper

salt to taste

3 tablespoons fresh dill

4 ounces sour cream

Melt butter in deep pot. Sauté vegetables until tender. Sprinkle flour over vegetables, continue cooking 1 minute.

Cut tomatoes in small chunks and add remaining ingredients to pot.

Simmer 10 minutes to allow flavors to blend.

Pour into bowls, add dill and a spoonful of sour cream.

ICE CREAM TO EAT IN A DISH AT HOME

CAPPUCCINO ICE CREAM
WITH BRANDY KAHLUA SAUCE

Ice Cream

3 large egg whites

4 tablespoons sugar

1 cup heavy cream

4 tablespoons sugar

1 tablespoon Kahlua

2 teaspoons instant coffee
 granules

Chopped coffee candy

Brandy Kahlua Sauce

1 cup water

3/4 cup sugar

1 tablespoons Cognac
 or brandy

1 tablespoon Kahlua

2 teaspoons instant coffee
 granules

Beat egg whites until foamy. Gradually add sugar; continue beating until whites are stiff and glossy.

In another bowl, whip cream with sugar until stiff. Dissolve coffee granules in Cognac and Kahlua; add to whipped cream. Mix well.

Combine egg whites with whipped cream mixture; blend well. Place in attractive, freezer-proof bowl. Top with coffee candy; freeze several hours.

To serve, place a mound in center of individual plate and surround with Brandy Sauce (see following recipe).

Continued . . .

To Make Brandy Sauce:

In small, deep saucepan, heat sugar and water over medium heat about 7 minutes until mixture is clear and syrupy-looking. Remove from heat. Stir in remaining ingredients. Allow to cool.

Note: Scoop ice cream into 12 paper-lined muffin cups; freeze. To serve, remove liners, place ice cream in stemmed glasses. Spoon over Brandy Sauce.

BARGAINING BROWNIES

MAKES 12 SQUARES

3 ounces unsweetened chocolate

1 cup (2 sticks) butter

2 cups sugar

1/4 teaspoon salt

4 eggs, slightly beaten

2 teaspoons vanilla

1/2 cup all-purpose flour

Melt chocolate with butter; blend well; stir in sugar; add salt, eggs and vanilla.

Sift flour over chocolate mixture; stir gently just until absorbed.

Pour batter into greased 9 x 9-inch pan. Set pan into larger pan filled 1/3 with very hot water. Place pans in upper 1/3 of oven.

Bake at 350° about 50 minutes until knife inserted near edge comes out clean and brownie-like crust is formed. Remove from water bath. Chill 2 to 3 hours before serving.

Top with whipped cream if desired.

SATURDAY MORNING SNACKS
TO HIDE FOR YOURSELF

PECAN CRUNCHIES

1 1/2 cups flour

4 tablespoons butter, cut into small pieces

1/2 teaspoon baking soda

1 tablespoon sugar

1/2 cup vanilla yogurt

2 tablespoons cinnamon sugar (optional)

1/4 cup chopped pecans

Using pastry blender, mix together first 4 ingredients until dough resembles coarse meal.

Add yogurt and pecans; blend until smooth. Form into large ball. Divide dough into 20 small balls. Flatten each ball with fork on lightly greased baking sheet; sprinkle with cinnamon sugar, if desired.

Bake at 400° about 12 minutes.

Serve warm.

Saturday Morning Snacks to Hide for Yourself

Cracker Snackers

35 soda crackers

1 cup butter

1 cup brown sugar, packed solid

1 cup chocolate chips

Grease a 17 x 11-inch baking sheet. Line bottom evenly with crackers. Do not overlap.

Combine butter and brown sugar in a heavy, non-stick saucepan. Cook over medium heat, stirring constantly until mixture comes to a boil. Continue cooking another 3 minutes, stirring constantly.

Pour mixture evenly over crackers

Bake at 375° for 15 minutes. Remove from oven and sprinkle with chocolate chips. Let stand a few minutes until chocolate melts. Spread evenly over crackers. Break into pieces. Chill in refrigerator until set.

SOMERSAULT SWEETIES

MAKES ABOUT 80 COOKIES

2 cups butter

1 1/2 teaspoon vanilla

1 cup + 2 tablespoons brown sugar, firmly packed

4 cups flour

1/2 teaspoon salt

Cream together butter and brown sugar until light and fluffy. Blend in vanilla.

Sift together flour and salt; gradually add to butter-sugar mixture; mix well. Chill dough 2 hours.

Shape dough into 1-inch balls; place about 2 inches apart on greased baking sheet. Flatten slightly with bottom of glass that has been dipped in sugar.

Bake at 325° about 12 minutes. Sprinkle with a little sugar. Cool on racks.

Tastes particularly good after exercising.

TARTS. NO EXPLANATION NECESSARY.

APPLE & APRICOT TART

1 ¾ cups all-purpose flour

1 teaspoon baking powder

3/4 cup sugar

1 1/2 sticks cold butter,
   cut into 24 pieces

2 tablespoons grated
   lemon peel

2 teaspoons lemon juice

1 cup chopped pecans

1 large egg, slightly beaten

1 cup sliced, peeled apples
   cut into bite-sized pieces

12 oz. apricot preserves

With pastry blender, mix together the first 4 ingredients until mixture resembles coarse meal.

Blend in the next 4 ingredients until a dough forms, mixing with hands if needed. Do not overbeat.

Divide the dough in half.

Spread the first half on the bottom of a greased 10-inch spring- . form pan, using floured fingers to spread dough evenly. Arrange apple slices over dough. Gently spread apricot preserves over apples.

With floured fingers, divide the remaining dough into 4 sections. Spread each into a large "leaf" and place on one-fourth

Continued . . .

of tart. Repeat with remaining dough so most of the surface is topped.

Bake at 350° for 35 minutes until golden. When cool, sprinkle on vanillan sugar* or powdered sugar.

Serves 12.

* Vanillan sugar can be found in the baking department of most grocery stores.

Tarts. No Explanation Necessary.

Pear Tart with Almond Cream

2 large pears, peeled, thinly sliced

Custard

2 eggs

1/3 cup cream

1/3 cup sour cream

1/3 cup sugar

1/3 cup finely ground
  almonds

1/2 teaspoon almond
  extract

Crust

1 1/2 cups sifted flour

1/3 cup sugar

1/2 cup finely ground
  almonds

1/2 cup softened butter

1 large egg

1 1/2 teaspoon almond
  extract

Jam

Almonds

Prepare *crust* by blending flour with sugar and almonds. Mix in butter until dough is like coarse meal. Beat together egg and extract. Add to dough mixture, blending well. Do not overbeat.

Pat mixture on bottom and sides of a greased 10-inch fluted tart pan (with removable bottom, if possible). Prick crust.

Continued . . .

Bake at 350° for 12 minutes until dough is fairly set. Set aside to cool.

Place pear slices in decorative pattern on bottom of baked crust. Beat together *custard* ingredients just until blended; pour over pears. Place pan on cookie sheet and bake at 350° for about 35 minutes. Set aside to cool.

When cool, glaze with jam and whole almonds.

Serves 8.